ViJayant

Flairs and Glairs
Publication House

"ViJayant"

ISBN No: " 978-93-90799-11-4"
1st Edition
Language – English and Hindi

Flairs and Glairs
Publication House
Regd. Under MSME Act.

Disclaimer

This is a work of fiction and solely represent the thoughts of the corresponding authors of the articles. Our editors have tried their best to edit the content of all the authors and check the plagiarism.
All the write-ups in this book are unique and are only published in this book.
In case any plagiarism or error is found, only the author is responsible alone, and not the publisher or the Compilers.

Cover Designing and Book Formatting
Shubham Shah and Ishani Agarwal

Acknowledgement

First of all, I thank God, for this life, as a human, has been a lesson full of experiences that have moulded me into the person I am today. To destiny, for teaching me lessons that no one else could.

I'd like to thank my parents for their support, without them, I'd be nothing. My sibling, Nishita Ninave, for her help, support and the blessing she is in my life.

I pay gratitude to my friends Avnish Kumar, Alolika Ray, Momo, Pavan Sharma, Ankita Kumar, and Anandhini Iyappan. You people are not just my friends but are my guiding angels who I know I can blindly rely upon.

Shubham Shah and the entire team of Flairs and Glairs, I salute your dedication and helping nature. You are the reason why the book was possible.

Last but not the least, all the co-authors who were extremely cooperative throughout the project. You all are the whole and soul of the book. All I wish is health and happiness for you all!

Co Author

Shubham Shah (Founder, Flairs And Glairs)
Ishani Agarwal (Co-Founder, Flairs And Glairs)
Grishma Ninave (Compiler)

1. Priyanshi Mittal
2. Sahina Ghugha
3. Deepti Bagde
4. Rajanish Tiwari
5. Pratima Yadav"Shaani"
6. Kalamkaar
7. Harsh Ninawe
8. Harshal Ninawe
9. Anand Kamal
10. Uzma Shakil
11. Krishna Motwani
12. Jeevitha.S
13. Keerthana Suriya
14. Trisha Banerjee
15. Hema Kirthiga J
16. Priyanka Ramakant Kadam
17. Priyanshi Rana
18. Ankit Srivastava
19. Krishan Kant Sen
20. Karan Nishad
21. Mansha Poddar
22. Vidhi Bhadreshbhai Desai
23. Sarabjot Purba
24. Foram Shah
25. Giftson Jose
26. Vishali.S

27. Rashmi Baweja
28. Shivani Bhardwaj
29. Jayashree Sahoo
30. S. Vasha Varthini
31. Sarbani Dey
32. Deepjyoti Chowdhury
33. Yamini Sona Vaishnavi
34. Amritanshu Shreshth
35. Abhilash Sharma
36. Sadhana Singh
37. Shivani Batra
38. Lakshmi Soni
39. Keshav Tibrewal
40. Anand Jain
41. Sarvesh Bagde
42. Bhavika Dhiraj Sindhi
43. Shivansh Sharma
44. Archana Paryani
45. Christy Gnana Deepa. J
46. Ipsita Panigrahi
47. Urja Motwani
48. R.Susanna Celsia
49. Ponmitha Selvaraj
50. Dhiraj Sindhi

Shubham Shah

(Founder- Flairs and Glairs)

Shubham Shah, an entrepreneur at "Flairs & Glairs" a brand with dynamics in events organizing and cultural educational pan INDIA, is a 26yrs old guy who recently has entered the digital platform of imprinting emotions. He has initiated with his own open mic platform to help budding poets and aspiring writers under his brand named as "Teekhe Zasbaaat"

He is a commerce graduate from the Bhagalpur City of Bihar. He states Writing has impersonated him since childhood and he has now been writing for over a decade!
Cooking, on the other hand, is his passion! He also mentions, trying out new things just tickles him!
When asked sir, Why SPICY EMOTIONS?
He smiled and added, "agar jasbaat teekhe na ho toh wo jasbaat kahan" Spices are all that blends! So do his words!
As a chef, he presents to you his dish! Hot and freshly served! Taste it! Feel it! Enjoy it! You can also find his writing in the Book "Teekhe Zasbaaat" and 50+ Co-authored anthologies. With his passion to explore opportunities across Platforms, he is working with keen devotion and We wish him all the very best for his future ventures.
He is Featured in the **International Magazine De-Mode** for his upcoming solo novel.
He is **Approved by Ne8x for its Lit Fest,** and is a **Golden Star Awards 2020 Winner.**
He is an **India Book of Records Holder** for his Anthology **Satrang,** and has the **Grandmaster** title by **Asia Book of Records**, for the same.
He has also been featured in **Prabhat Khabar**, **Dainik Jagran** and other renowned Newspaper for his achievements. He has also been awarded with **India Star Republic Award 2021.**
He has been a proud co-author to
India Book of Records (Title- Black)
World Book of Records (Title -15 Wonders of Poetries)
India Book of Records (Title - Aaina)
Vajra World Records Holder (Title - Gustakhi Maaf Hai)
High Range of Records Holder (Title - Gustakhi Maaf Hai)

Share your reviews on his

INSTAGRAM

@spicy_emotions
@shubham4shah

Or via email on

shubham2shah@gmail.com

To stay tuned to his work and opportunities follow his business Handles

INSTAGRAM FACEBOOK YOUTUBE

@flairsandglairs
@teekhezasbaaat

WEBSITE:

https://flairsandglairs.in/
https://flairsandglairs.com/

Ishani Agarwal

(Co-Founder- Flairs and Glairs)

Ishani Agarwal hails from the City of Joy, Kolkata.
She is the co-founder of her Community "Teekhe Zasbaaat" and Flairs and Glairs Publication.
Been a Compiler for 45+ Anthologies, she is in the process for more. Co-authored in 150+ Anthologies. She is a India Book of Records Holder, a Vajra World Records Holder, a High Range of Records Holder and a Bravo Record holder.

Approved by Ne8x for its Lit Fest 2020, and Literary Icon 2020. Also a Golden Star Awards Winner 2020.
She has also been awarded with India Star Republic Award 2021.
She has been featured by the National Magazine "Taree Zameen Par" with the title 'unstoppable'.
Also featured in the International Magazine DeMode for her upcoming solo novel, she is proud to write on social issues, and is happy with the love she is receiving.
Connect with her on Instagram: @Ishani_agarwal_quotes / @compilations_so_far

Grishma Ninave

(Compiler)

A student of science and an admirer of arts.
A science graduate cherishing the art of writing, working as a project head at Flairs & Glairs Publication House. Published in the Editorial section of a national magazine as Aaj Ki Womaniyaa, in the first edition of 2021.
A minion millenial with extra-large dreams.
Is in active rebellion with her mother about the number of books she must have in the house.

When not reading, can be found writing and reviewing books a lot.
Firm believer that music is what can revive and reconcile the world.
She's one of those people who love greys more than colours and she's like a colourful autumn too at the same time.
Admires old school love stories and retro music.
A Capricorn girl who believes hearts are more important than physical appearances.
Is into deep talks with a very few people, but believes they are the driving force of joy in her life.
Loves traveling to places where there are mountains, trees, hills and treks.
No wonder nature's beauty strikes a chord within her.
The guiding light in her life is the quote, "Don't search for happiness, because it's not something you find, it's something you create!"

Has participated in around 150 anthologies and compiled a few titles too.

Smile

Smile,
Despite the pain pulling you down,
And despite the battles you have won.
Smile, like it is your weapon.

Smile,
After losing your love,
And after losing yourself to love.
Smile, like it is your heart.

Smile,
When you have had a bad day,
And when you make someone else's better.
Smile, like it is your good.

Smile,
While you soak your pillow crying,
And while you're dancing.
Smile, like it is your music.

एक बरसात अभी बाकी है।।

सूखा पड़ा है मन आँगन,
हवाओं में आग काफ़ी है।
दर्द के सूरज का तपा पिघलाने आनी,
एक बरसात अभी बाकी है।।

सालों से जलते आँखों के पानी को,
हर जले को भीगाने के लिए।
कुछ साज़िशों से भरे हालात बाकी है,
एक बरसात अभी बाकी है।।

अँधेरे से भरी इन गलियों में,
आनी एक प्रभात बाकी है।
कोने में बैठी बेरुखी को भिगाने आनी,
एक बरसात अभी बाकी है।।

बरसों सताया जिस दूरी ने,
एक रिझाने के लिए एक मुलाक़ात काफ़ी है।
आँखों को मुस्कुराहट दे जाए ऐसी,
एक बरसात अभी बाकी है।।

मुर्दों की तरह रहते इससे टूटे दिल में,
आनी अभी हयात बाकी है।
नई शुरुआत से पहले दुनिया को धोने वाली,
एक बरसात अभी बाकी है।।

Priyanshi Mittal

Priyanshi. An enthusiastic writer.
An eternal optimist, dreamer, and a student with a flair for writing
Creative writing and poetry are what she likes doing in her spare time...
And she believes that life is a journey with vivid twists and turns to be explored in every moment.

Raindrop

When I was coming down
Saw Greenland in a town
Saw a girl on her knees
Shading tears continuously
When I asked what had happened
No reply but stand straightened
She replied lack of mother
I said don't bother
God gives a bright star as mother
Lives everywhere as no one can other
Her smile is simple
Having a simple
Her eyes are blue with a lovely view
Glad to see on her face
After a long decade

नारी शक्ति

जब जन्म लिया तो आंचल से मां ने मुझको था ढक कर रखा
छू लुंगी वो आसमा इरादा था मेरा भी पक्का
इस दुनिया को दिखलाना था ,कुछ इनको भी समझाना था
समझे ना कोई फर्क जरा तो ,उनको भी बतलाना था
लड़की अब कोई कमजोर नहीं, चलता उसपर अब जोर नहीं
कुदरत को अब तुम पहचान लो ,बात मेरी ये मान लो
पैदा अब हर लड़की होगी, उन जल्लादो की कड़की होगी
सिर्फ़ मेरी नहीं-२
हर लड़की की आजादी होगी ,अंध विश्वास के उन पुतलों की मानो
अब बर्बादी होगी
हर लड़की की आजादी होगी।

Sahina Ghugha

Sahina Ghugha is a 20-year-old b.com student at Saurashtra University Rajkot. She is from Jamnagar city of Gujarat. She is a state-level winner in poetry competition 2017. She is Co-author of 10+ anthologies. She is an amazing writer and poet and she wants to do something for society through her pen.
Instagram ID:- Itz_Sahina_write

खोल दो दिल पर लगे, ज़ंग खा चुके तालों को,
साफ़ करो इसमें लग गए मकड़ी के जालों को।
खोल दो खिड़कियां, अंदर आने दो उजालों को,
उतार फैको जिस्म पर लगी, यादों की ख़ालो को।
फ़िर से नई मुस्कान लेकर, तुम सबको चौंका दो,
तुम्हारी ही ज़िन्दगी है, इसे हसने का दूसरा मौका दो।

खुद पर लगाई है जो बंदिशे, अब उनको तोड़ दो,
पूरी करने अपनी ख्वाहिशें, गम का रास्ता छोड़ दो।
कैद कर रखी है खुशियां जिसमें, वो गुल्लक फोड़ दो,
छोड़ सारी शिकायतें, खुद को लापरवाही से जोड़ दो।
ज़िन्दगी के समंदर में गम का तूफ़ान पार करने नौका दो,
तुम्हारी ही ज़िन्दगी है, इसे हसने का दूसरा मौका दो।

Deepti Bagde

Deepti Bagde is from Antagarh, dist-Kanker (Chhattisgarh). She is a Co-author of 5 anthologies. She is an amazing writer. She wants to spread positivity in society through her pen.

हौसला

दिल जो चाहे,मिल ना पाए।
क्यूं भला!क्यूं भला?
क्यूं भला हम छोड़ सारे ग़म।खुली हवा में सांस ना लें,क्यूं ना हम
मुस्कुराएं,भूल के सारे शिकवे गिला।
दिल जो चाहे मिल ना पाए ।
क्यूं भला!क्यूं भला।
उम्मीदों का दामन थामे हम,आशाओं के पर से क्यों ना उड़ें।
तोड़ें हमें सभी,क्यों ना चाहे कोई, आत्मविश्वास से हम जुड़ें।
क्यूं हमेशा सुने हम सबकी,पर सुने ना दिल की सदा।
दिल जो चाहे मिल ना पाए,क्यूं भला !क्यूं भला?
देखे जो सपने आसमान के, क्यूं हमें कोई रोक जाता है।
छूना चाहें गर आकाश को , कोई जमी पर ले ही आता है।
छोड़ दुजों को खुद से कह दो अब,
तुम्हारी मुठ्ठी में है जहां।
तुम भी पा सकते हो ख्वाहिशों से भरा वो आसमां।
छू ले तू आसमां ,छा जा तू हर जगह।
कि देखता रह जाए सारा जहां।
खुद पर रख बस हौसला।

मेरा मुकाम

मेरे सपने हैं बहुत ऊंचे,
उससे भी ऊंचा है मेरा मुकाम।
है तकदीर पर भरोसा इतना ,
मेरे लिए है सारा आसमान।
आज नहीं तो कल, जिऊंगी वो पल ।
जो है सिर्फ मेरा, बनाएगा मुझे जो सफल।
न सिर्फ पाऊंगी बेहतर मुकाम ,
पर पूरा करूंगी सबके अरमान।
क्यूंकि मेरे सपने है ,ऊंचे बहुत ।
और उनसे भी ऊंचा है मेरा मुकाम।

Rajanish Tiwari

Rajanish Tiwari
M.Sc. (Biotechnology)
Writes to express emotions

Email: rajnishtiwari1996@gmail.com
Instagram: rajanish_tiwari_

कर के दिखाऊँगा...।

मंजिल मेरी तय है उसे पूरा करके ही सो पाऊँगा,
अपने लक्ष्य को पूरा कर के दिखाऊँगा ।

ना मंजिल ना शोहरत ना ही किसी दौलत के लिए,
बस माँ तेरी सूरत पे रौनक के लिए
मैं जान पे खेल जाऊंगा,
अपने लक्ष्य को पूरा कर के दिखाऊँगा ।

चाहे आए मुश्किल हजार या टूटे गमों का पहाड़,
हर मुसीबत को मैं अपनी मेहनत से हराऊँगा
अपने लक्ष्य को पूरा कर के दिखाऊँगा ।

सब ने दिए धोखे हजार उठ कर खड़ा हुआ में हर बार,
अब होने ही वाला है वो चमत्कार
जब जीत से मचा दूंगा मैं हाहाकार ।
जीत का नगाड़ा अब बजा के दिखाऊँगा,
अपने लक्ष्य को पूरा कर के दिखाऊँगा ।

टूटे दिल की दास्तान ।

कसूर है किसका ? तेरा, मेरा या हालातों का ?
चुना तूने ही तो था, जुदाई का रास्ता...।

छोड़ा जो तूने मुझे तन्हा,
अब सीख लिया मैंने तेरे बिना जीने का तरीका
टूटा-रोया चैन और सुकून खोया,
पर हारा नहीं मैं जानेजाँ ।

अब नफरत तो नहीं कर सकता
पर कर लिया है ये फैसला,
तुम्हें भूलकर मैंने चुना है जीने का मकसद नया ।

अब सीख गया हूं मैं जीना तन्हा तेरे बिना,
अब तुम आओ तो क्या ? ना आओ तो क्या..?

Pratima Yadav "Shaani"

Shaani... An MBBS student and a part-time writer... quite passionate about reading novels and writing especially poetry and song lyrics. Ambitious optimistic and extrovert person. Going to be a published author soon. Contact her at yadavpratimayaduvanshi@gmail.com
Instagram account @itsshaani

लम्हा गुज़र जाएगा...

कुछ कह था दिया
कुछ रह सा गया
कतरा कतरा करके ही सही
वो लम्हा गुज़र ही गया
कुछ को भुला दिया
कुछ ने भुला दिया
कतरा कतरा करके ही सही
वो लम्हा गुज़र ही गया

वो लम्हा जब अन्धेरे थे
वो लम्हा जब कहीं दूर उजाले थे
वो लम्हा जब अपने पराये थे
वो लम्हा जब हम बेगाने थे
वो लम्हा जब खो गये साए थे
वो लम्हा जब सारी रात रोये थे
कतरा कतरा करके ही सही
वो लम्हा गुज़र ही गया
आज फिर सवेरा आया है
आज फिर अपनों ने गले लगाया है..
तन्ज कसने वाले आज प्यार कर रहे हैं ..जिंदगी के पहलु तो अब बदल रहे हैं
पराये भी आज अपना रहे हैं
अपने तो खैर अपने हैं
टुकड़ों मे कर के ही सही
अंधेरा सिमट ही गया
कतरा कतरा करके ही सही
वो लम्हा गुज़र ही गया।

Kalamkaar

This is Kalamkaar. He is from Uttarakhand bought up in Meerut(Up). His hobbies are reading and writing. His interest is in writing. He loves writing. He is part of 295 +Anthologies as a Co-Author. He won 290 + Certificate in Writing, He started writing on 29 February 2020. He is part of 2 anthologies as Co-Author going for the record and He is OMG record holder as Co-Author of Book Called Laposia. He is part of 5 international Anthologies as a Co-Author. He is a simple and people observer. His Instagram handle is kalamkaar51 and his email is kalamkaar51@gmail.com. He believes in Karma.

सकारात्मक रहें

आये कितनी भी मुश्किल रहा मे।
ना डरे ना अपना उत्साह खोये।
जो करना हैं सफल होने मे।
अपने लक्ष्य तक पहुंचने के लिए प्रयास करें।
ना हो हताश अपने अंदर ऊर्जा को करें उत्पन्न।
ना हो असफल और कार्य सारे हो सम्पन।
रखे अपने अंदर हौसला, करते जाये कार्य।
रखे भरोसा अपने अंदर, होगा तुम्हारा जो लिया ख़ुद के लिए फैसला।
मिलेगी सफलता एक ना एक दिन तुमको।
और होंगे सारे काम पूरे जो छोड़े अधूरे।
किया नहीं भरोसा जिसने और करा तुम्हारे हौसले को नीचे।
बनो इतने सफल जो लोग तुम्हारी तरफ आ जाये खींचे।
उठाना ना कदम वो जिससे तुम्हें हो नुक्सान।
करना कड़ी मेहनत क्योकि होता नहीं सफलता पाने का रास्ता आसान।
आ जाये कितने उतार चढ़ाव मत करना अपने पे सवाल।
क्योकि वो तुम सबसे बढ़िया और हो तुम बाकमाल।
हालातो से हारकर मत सोचना नकारात्मक
करना भरोसा खुदपे और अपनी काबिलयत पर रहना हमेशा सकारात्मक।

Harsh Ninawe

He is studying at Shri Shivaji Science College, Nagpur.
His hobbies are bike riding, playing cricket, cooking, playing badminton, listening to songs.

1)जिवनात खूप मोठे चढ उतार येतात, त्याला 'सामोरे जाणे 'हे आपल्या हातात असतं .

2)माणूस पैशाने नाही तर " मनाने " मोठं पाहिजे .

3)आयुष्य खुप सुंदर आहे पण त्याला कश्याप्रकारे जगायचं हे आपल्या हातात आहे .

4) आयुष्य हे एक " आईस-क्रिम " सारखं आहे .
एक तर ' टेस्ट ' करा नाहीतर ' वेस्ट ' .

5) ज्याप्रकारे शेतात बिज पेरल्याशिवाय फळ मिळत नाही ,
त्याचप्रकारे कष्ट केल्याशिवाय ' यश ' मिळत नाही .

6) आयुष्याचा पुस्तकाचं फक्त दोन पान रंगवले आहेत
पहिलं ' जन्म ' आणि
दुसरं ' मृत्यु '
आता मधातलं रिकाम पान भरणे हे आपल्या हातात आहे.

7) आयुष्यात खूप श्रीमंत व्हा पण ' पैशाने ' नाही तर ' मनाने '

Harshal Ninawe

She studied at S .N. Mor College Tumsar.
She likes reading books, cooking.

1) जिंकण्याची तयारी तिथूनच करायची, जिथे हरण्याची जास्त भीती वाटते .

2) पराभवाची भिती बाळगू नका एक ' मोठा विजय ' तुमचे सर्व पराभव पुसुन टाकू शकतो .

3) आयुष्य हा एक बुद्धीबळाचा खेळ आहे , जर टिकून राहायचे असेल तर चाल स्त्पत राहाव्या लागतात .

4) भरलेला खिसा माणसाला दुनिया दाखवतो ,
रिकामा खिसा मात्र दुनियेतील माणसं दाखवतो .

5) आयुष्यात एकदा तरी वाईट दिवसांना सामोरे गेल्याशिवाय दिवसांची किंमत कळत नाही.

6) परिस्थिती गरीब असली तरी चालेल पण ,विचार मात्र ' भिकारी ' नसावेत .

7) जिंकण्याची मजा तेव्हाच येते , जेव्हा लोक तुमच्या हरण्याची वाट पाहत असतात .

Anand Kamal

Anand Kamal is one of the names among young amazing writers. He is a very good poetry writer who used to write on present situations and scenarios describing reality. He is a sportive, supportive, young, writer who loves bike riding, traveling, and helping others.

You can contact him on his email id
Anandgp1999@gmail.com

Kabhi kuch khamoshiya shor kar jaati hai...
Kabhi kuch majbooriya kamjor kar jaati hai...
Chaho kitna khud ko majboot rakhlo...
Par kabhi kuch pal bahut rulaati hai...
Kabhi yaadein bahut satati hai…
To kabhi najdikiya ander se tod jaati hai...
Kabhi apna saya bhi saath chudaati hai...
Kabhi humsafar bhi saath chod jaati hai...
Kabhi khamosh najre bhi aasuwo ka sailaab bahati hai...
Kabhi muskurahat bhi saath chod jaati hai...
Kabhi khudse khudko bhagati hai...
Kabhi anchahe khwaab bankar tadpaati hai...
Ye khamoshiya bhi bahut sor machati hai...
Toote dilo k haal muskurahato se chupaati hai...
Jalte angaaro me bhi paani sa ehsaas karati hai...
Kuch jimmedaariyo ka ehsaas bachpana cheen le jaati hai...
Kabhi kuch ankahein jazbaat cheekhti chillati hai...
Toote sapno se har baar ek nayi tasveer banati hai...
Bichde apno k khone k ehsaas har baar karati hai...
Ye khamoshiya hai ...bahut shor machaati hai...

Waqt se ladkar waqt ko hi harana hai...
Zinda hu me abhi ye baat zamane ko batlana hai...
Un khwaabo ko haqiqat banana hai...
Un toote armaano ko firse sajana hai...
Aaj phir khoyi bulandiyo ko paana hai...
Un khoye lamho ko aaj phir bulana hai...
Toote sapno se aaj phir ek tasveer banana hai...
Bichde apno ko phir aaj pana hai...
Jaleel huye har ek lamho ka hissab chukana hai...
Me Zinda hu abhi zinda najar aana hai...
Phir safaltao k sikhar pe aana hai...
Mujhe har ek toote shaksh me ek Atoot ANAND banana hai...
Mujhe aaj phir khud me Khud ko paana hai...
Khud ko khud k hone ka ehsaas karana hai...
Me bheed nahi hu duniya ka mere ander bhi ek jamana hai...
Me bheed nahi hu duniya ka mere ander bhi ek jamana hai...
Mere ander bhi ek jamana hai.

Uzma Shakil

Uzma is a student and aspires to become a doctor. She is a nature lover and has learned many things from it. She believes that everything has a positive side. Her aim in life is to serve the needy and open an orphanage for poor homeless children. She writes about the current situation of the world and she is a good speaker as well.

The Beauty Of Existence

Moon is lonely but beautiful.
But who says it's the only beauty in the universe,
For the star shines upon me and becomes a poem to my life.
Heaven is heaven because of its boundlessness,
but honestly one needs angles in hell, not in heaven.
That milky way and this earth meets at the horizon of togetherness.
The sun suspended above burns itself for my heart to melt.
Space carrier all the rocks and boulders so that my life goes smooth.
The flowers spread their fragrance and make my day a delightful one.
The waterfall shows the positivity of downfall,
Colourful butterflies make my world a fairytale,
And my people makes me feel safe.
This earth is a home to me and I am its child.

Krishna Motwani

Krishna Motwani is a Student currently.
She uses to pen down her feelings.
She is a moody girl.
She started writing in the month of June 2020.
She writes in her free time.
She writes some motivational quotes or poetry too and practices artworks also.
She lives her life like a bird
As a bird flies freely and enjoys life like that she also lives her life freely and enjoys the fullest.

I Expect!

I expect India should be free of rituals.
All Indians should think positive always.
Society should not discriminate between girls and boys.
All of us should give equal rights to everyone.
A girl should be free to go outside at night.
Boys should not tease any of the girls.
Most of the people think that girl shouldn't take birth, they kill the girl if she takes birth, that should be stopped because we are here only and only because of girls!!
All of us shouldn't believe in superstitions.
Rape should be stopped in this whole world.
All these worst things should be stopped then our India will change fully!

I expect that God will accept my expectations
And India will change soon!

Jeevitha. S

She is a girl with stupendous writing skills. Her heart is a castle abound with unbreakable courage, being contained with enticing dreams. Penning is her way of spreading aesthetic vibes among her readers. Being a literarian is her pride. She loves to be a unicorn amidst the flock of sheep!

Unflinching Belief Upon Life!

Although she walked through her darkest days,
She always had a glimmer in her eyes.
She believed in something which was unseen and unheard,
That one thing was her hope on the whole;
She edified something new in all that she went through,
She became aesthetic on the whole,
Miracle does happen at the end ;
When she rejuvenated her soul through her hope.
There exists the glide of positive vibes,
She summoned more wisdom and insight.
All her dejections flew away ;
And her eyes once again shimmered with jubilance.
Accepting struggles and proceeding furthermore,
Her puzzles were solved through her beliefs about life.

Keerthana Suriya

She is Ms.Keerthana Suriya a highly aspired, dynamic medical student, social-worker, passionate writer, and classical dancer who is engaging in self and social development, building relationships, and exhibiting integrity. She is Co-Author of various other anthologies. She is the Founder of WACHC Foundation - Women And Children Health Care and also holding the position of Women's Health Empowerment Project Head in the trust Women's Renaissance Centre. She strongly believes that "When women and children rise, their communities and countries rise with them". Follow her on Instagram - @keethusm

Quit

If the word 'quit' is
popping up in your mind, it means
it is sending a message
about your fear of failure
Fear will paralyze you
if you do not deal with it
Overcome your fear of failure
If you want to live life to its fullest
you have to take the risk of failure
QUIT
Quit your thoughts about quitting
Confront negative thoughts and
circumstances and maintain a
positive attitude.
To try and fail is really not a failure
It is actually a kind of success
But to wilt and stop is failure
Overcome the fear of failure
SUCCEED

Trisha Banerjee

Trisha Banerjee is a person who gives an equal weightage to her heart and brain and stands by the right decision in her life. She is a passionate, promising perfectionist. Music, food, and dogs are her major turn-ons. Keeping her dreams, the first priority she goes on in her life like an unstoppable storm.

Motivation Is The Key To Win

Motivation is an attitude that grooms a person's character. Everybody sets their own happy goals in life and dreams to fulfill those aspirations. To reach the desired destination, one needs to focus, work hard and have patience. A person can put in such an effort only and only if he/she is highly motivated. You must be transparent to yourself. Talking to yourself will always help you to find out the solutions to all your problems. Sit down, close your eyes and say "I am the best and I will do it ". Believe what you say so that your inner voice also says it loud and clear. If your inner voice is loud enough then no voice can silent you. Success is not always constant. Failures are a part of life. Failing teaches us to rise like a Phoenix. A strong comeback after an excruciating setback is the true stage where the power of your motivation is tested. Don't think about what will happen if you work hard but think that what will happen if you do not work hard. A highly motivated person should also prevent himself/herself from walking on negative paths like- jealousy, dishonesty, procrastination, etc. The 3 B's you need to follow in your life are-Breathe, Believe and Begin. I would like to end by sharing a quote of APJ Abdul Kalam which is one of my best-loved quotes- "Failure will never overtake me if my definition to succeed is."

Hema Kirthiga J

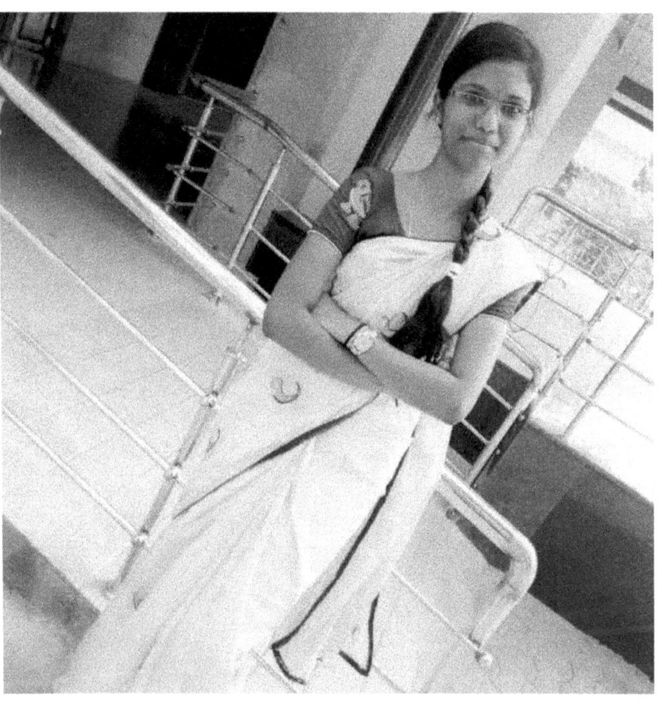

She is Hema Kirthiga J, and her pen name is sparkle. She is professionally a psychologist and passionately a writer. She heals others but writing heals her. She is a writer, reader, orator, and a believer. She is from Chennai. She lives by the principle of inspire and be inspired.

Instagram- @the_pen_queen
Email- inker.sparkle@gmail.com
Yourquote – JKM

Be Positive!!

What is life?
Isn't it with ups and downs,
Isn't it an adventure,
That we want to venture,
Our life is a vehicle,
Which runs with positivity,
Fuel it up,
And run,
Achieve what you desire,
Win and shine,
Don't be reckless,
And fuel it with negativity,
Then your life will blast,
Don't let the failure,
Pause your life,
Let you shine,
Bright and high,
Fight with all the might,
Be positive,
That's all it matters.

Priyanka Ramakant Kadam

She writes from the heart what you relate and her heart says. She feels every moment of life that she pen down through her writing which she felt with the heart.

Professionally she wants to be a developer but her dreams are so big and one of her dreams is to explore as a writer as it inspires her a lot towards the journey of her better life.

She loves to explore more and more...That's what her life is...

जीवन को स्वीकार करो
हर परिस्थिति को समझा करो,
अपना रास्ता खुद खोंजा करो,
जितना हे उतने मैं जिया करो
और की अपेक्षा मत करो,
हमेशा खुश रहना का प्रयास करो,
जीवन के कुछ पहलू को जाना करो,
काँटे हों या फूल
करो ज़िन्दगी को क़ुबूल
क्योंकि यह अपनी समग्रता और वास्तविकता में,
जो वास्तविकता के साथ एकांत
और आगे बढ़ने के बारे में,
कभी-कभी आपको केवल वास्तविकता
को स्वीकार करना होगा
और बस आगे बढ़ना होगा,
क्योंकि कभी-कभी यह
समझने के लिए नहीं
बल्कि होने के लिए होता,
तो स्थिति जो भी हो उसे स्वीकार करो,
पर तुम कभी ना रूखना
बस आगे बढ़ते रहना,
फिर चाहिए हार भी क्यों ना आए
तुम हताश ना होना,
हमेशा सकारात्मक
और मुस्कुराते रहना,
एक दिन तुम जरूर जीत जाओगे,
पर यकीन रखो तुमे
जीवन में जो भी चाहिए
वह मिल जाएगा...
बस अंत तक जीवन में
अपना प्रयास जारी रखना...

Priyanshi Rana

A published writer; from Surat, Gujarat. Love to write pragmatic content, eumoirous, love to explore in the majestic ocean, an artist, enjoy traveling, fondness in poems, quotes, stories & more exhilarative content...have much more eagerness to write on current topics(people's voice).

Life a quite a difficult path,
But leads to many beautiful relations and moments,
The main requirement is to love and to be loved,
It doesn't ask you to be the best,
It just asks you to try your best,
Just live the moment like it will never come again,
Just see through your heart,
Because eyes don't see what you require to be happy,
Just live in the present because it will soon become a regretful past.

The rule of life is,
That never invest your feelings,
If you have not considered,
Face every worst outcome,
There are many rules,
For living a successful life,
The second one is to,
Understand that, l
This life is a one-time chance,
Don't waste it, It is not a problem,
It is just an experience.

Ankit Srivastava

अंकित श्रीवास्तव
जन्म एवं कर्म भूमि: रायबरेली (उत्तर प्रदेश)
कार्य: शोध छात्र
शौक: हिंदी काव्य साहित्य एवं संस्कृति में विशेष रुचि सहित अंशकालिक लेखन

खुद पर काम करो

कुछ ऐसा तुम काम करो
जग में तुम अपना नाम करो
बढ़ते चलो अपने लक्ष्य की ओर
तनिक न तुम विश्राम करो,
थोड़ा खुद पर काम करो...
तुम एक अच्छे इंसान बनो
सपनों में अपने जान भरो
बने जो तुम्हारे लक्ष्य की बाधा
उस शक्ति को नाकाम करो,
थोड़ा खुद पर काम करो...
न किसी को तुम बदनाम करो
तुम स्वयं में एक इतिहास बनो
न झुको कभी किसी के आगे तुम
बस कर्म को अपने प्रणाम करो,
थोड़ा खुद पर काम करो...
करो परिश्रम इतना की तुम
हक में अपने हर परिणाम करो
अपनी कमियों को दूर करो तुम,
बस थोड़ा खुद पर काम करो...!

उदास न होना

जिंदगी में कभी उदास न होना
बस अपने पथ पर ही चलते रहना
कुछ ख्वाब तुम्हारे टूटेंगे मगर
बिन सपनों के तुम कभी न सोना,
जिंदगी में कभी उदास न होना...
तुम अपने मन में दृढ़ निश्चय करना
असफलता से कभी हताश न होना
मुश्किलें तो बहुत आएंगी मगर
चेहरे से अपने मुस्कान न खोना,
जिंदगी में कभी उदास न होना...
जीना तुम अपनी ही शर्तों पर
होकर निर्भर स्वयं के कंधों पर
डिग जाए गर कदम तुम्हारे फिर भी
तुम कभी भी आत्मविश्वास न खोना,
जिंदगी में कभी उदास न होना...!

Krishan Kant Sen

कहानियों से कहानी का सृजन करने वाले "कृष्ण कान्त सेन", राजस्थान के छोटे से शहर बाराँ से आते है। उनकी रचनायें अंग्रेजी व हिन्दी, दोनो भाषाओं में मिलती हैं। सगुण भक्ति धारा को आदर्श मानने वाले "कृष्ण कान्त" की काव्य रचनाओं में माधुर्य व ओज का विशेष प्रभाव है।

अंग्रेजी भाषा से परास्नातक होने के साथ ही लेखन के अतिरिक्त फोटोग्राफी में भी विशेष रुचि रखते हैं।

कीका

माँ नें दिया था नाम जिसे कीका।
रंग पड़ा न जिसका कभी फीका।

रण में भयंकर,था अति बलशाली।
दो हाथों में थी दो तलवार सम्भाली।
साठ किलो का भाला लेकर,
रण में प्रचण्ड वेग बनकर,
मुगलों पर कड़ा प्रहार किया।
मेवाड़ी सेना में नव जोश संचार किया।

मेवाड़ी आन बचाने को,
अकबर का शीश झुकाने को,
रजपूतों ने केसरिया धार लिया।
मेवाड़ी सेना नें भीषण हुंकार किया।
रक्तपात फिर हुआ जमकर,
मुगल पड़े थे धरती पर,
हल्दीघाटी सनी खून से,
वीर लड़े निज जमीं चूम कर,
झाला-माना नें अपना विस्तार किया।
मुगलों नें डर से फिर चीत्कार किया।

मुठ्ठी भर सेना मेवाड़ी,
धधक रही थी जो चिंगारी,
परबस नही अब होना है,
जान भले दे देना है,
जंगल में रहना स्वीकार किया।
पराधीनता को इनकार किया।
कहानी अब आगे की सुनो भाई!

राणा नें फिर रोटी घाँस की खाई।
भूखे रहना स्वीकार किया,
भामाशाह नें धन समस्त दान किया,
सेना को फिर तैयार किया,
शस्त्रों को फिर धार दिया।
मुगलों पर धावा बोल दिया,
मुगलों का आसन डोल गया,
भाग पड़े मुगल फिर से दिल्ली,
मानों सिंह को देख भागे बिल्ली,
दिवेर की चौकियों पर राणा का अधिकार हुआ।
मेवाड़ी मान का नित विस्तार हुआ।

मेवाड़ धरा का मतवाला, राणा प्रताप चेतक वाला है।
झाला-माना और भामाशाह भी, आन बचाने वाला है।

Karan Nishad

Karan Nishad, 21 years old from Mumbai. With the dream of exploring the world of his imagination. He is also in search of his existence in the world of poetry with some blank pages of his diary.

Take Some Time

Take some time off to self-reflect and
self-measure
Sometimes you need to be
self-centered
To understand yourself better
I'm feeling self-possessed without the selfishness of self-
obsession
But if I do this for myself and no one else, then it is self-
expression
Self-confident,
in that, I'll never let myself forfeit
Because every word I write,
I'm certain,
I'm just painting a self-portrait

I pray

Kindly keep me from brokenness.
If it's not truly for me
then let these hopes vanish,
and the feelings that penetrate
inside my head for hours.
Don’t let me fall and drown deep so when it leaves
I'll be happy leaving the waters and go back to the shore
where I once found it.
Don't let me hold on to the story if it isn't mine,
if it isn't real and if it won’t last.
Please, don't let me.
And I hate it somehow
to say that I love it,
I love it in a thousand unsaid ways.
But I also pray
that if its mine and real,
and if it lasts a lifetime
only Him knows
how much I love it, and
how much my heart rejoices.

Mansha Poddar

Mansha Poddar was born on 14th August 2003 in Sambalpur, Odisha. Since childhood, her parents and teachers have supported her in her writing skills. She is a sprouting bud of fantasy who loves to dress up her words. She aspires to become a well-known writer as well as a Forest Officer. You can reach her for more of her scribbled writings on Instagram at @perpetual_covet

Known Strangers

Meeting someone online might add spice to life,
Sometimes old relations also revive.
It happened when I accidentally met my friend,
We turned from known strangers to infinity strength.
After that separation, it was our first happiness,
We gave all the time to each other and enhance.
Love and friendship have changed a lot,
We are tied in a stronger bond and never keep a clot.
It feels more understanding than the old-time,
We never leave a chance to make each other shine.
We were strangers when she joined my school,
But now we are the breeze of atmosphere so cool.

Everything happens for a reason. Even if you cried last night or you are happy at this moment it's for a reason. No matter, You believe it or not but this is a fact. Your every action your every word can affect someone very deeply. That's why the choice of words is very crucial whenever you speak. It depicts your personality.
Think about it.

Vidhi Bhadreshbhai Desai

Teacher by profession and writer by passion Vidhi loves to write her heart out in simple language...

बस कर्म किए जा

ज़िन्दगी से रख ना कोई ऊमीद बस कर्म किए जा,
ना डर मुश्केलियो से बस होंसला बनाके आगे बढ़ते जा।।
माना मुश्किल हैं डगर और न हैं कोई हमसफर,
फिरभी तू अपने कदम उठाए जा।।
मिलेगा जो तेरे नसीब में लिखा है किसी न किसी तरह,
बस रख अपने खुदा पे भरोसा और उसकी इबादत किए जा।।
ज़िन्दगी से रख ना कोई ऊमीद बस कर्म किए जा,
ना डर मुश्केलियो से बस होंसला बनाके आगे बढ़ते जा।।

The Life I Wanna Live

Dream of a life you want to live,
Pursue on your way towards its door...
And thy you will know the way of life,
The way you wanna live...

Dream big and work hard,
At last, what matters is the VICTORY you always wanna see,
And thy you will know the way of life,
The way you wanna live...

Dream of the dream you always dream,
Dream the life you want it to be,
At last, what matters is the life of dream,
You always wanna live...
And thy you will know the way of life,
The way you wanna live,
The way you wanna live...

Sarabjot Purba

सरबजोत पुरबा कोटकपूरा, पंजाब में रहते है। जब वो बारवीं कक्षा में थे तब उन्होंने पहली बार एक कविता लिखी। इसके बाद ई.टी.टी. की पढ़ाई करते समय उन्होंने कविताओं के साथ-साथ निबंध और कहानी भी लिखनी शुरू की। उन्होंने ने अपने मन के विचारो को एक किताब का रूप दिया है। जिसका नाम 'कुछ विचार' है। उन्होंने ई.टी.टी. कालेज का समय भी लिखा है। जिसमें उन सभी यादो को लिखा है जो उन्होंने ई.टी.टी. में बनाई थी। उन्होंने हर विषय पर कुछ न कुछ लिखा है। अक्सर वो समाज के मुद्दों पर लिखते है। वे ज्यादातर पंजाबी भाषा का प्रयोग करते है।

संघर्ष और जिन्दगी

कुछ पाना है तो,
मेहनत भी करनी चाहिए।
मंजिल एक बार ना मिले तो,
आहे नहीं भरनी चाहिए।
तुम इतने बहादुर हो,
किस्मत भी तुमसे डरनी चाहिए।
खुद को कमजोर मत बनने दो,
सीढ़ी मंजिल की चढ़नी चाहिए।

संघर्ष तो करना होगा,
देखना, तुम सबको हरा दोगे।
अब आराम ना किया तो,
जिन्दगी भर आराम लोगे।
नींद से प्यार छोड़दो,
आगे जाकर खूब सोगे।
काम को बोझ मत समझना,
तुम अवश्य कामयाब होगे।

यह जिन्दगी तुम्हारी है,
तुम ही इसे बदल पाओगे।
अगर कुछ करने का जज्बा हो,
तो पहाड़ भी हिलाओगे।
माँ-बाप का कर्ज है तुम पर,
सफल होकर कर्ज लुटाओगे।
संघर्ष ही एक जरिया है,
जिससे खुद को तुम चमकाओगे।

Foram Shah

Her name is Foram Shah. She belongs to Mumbai. She is happy to go girl and always ready to help people. Poetry is her way of expression and she dreams to be a great poet. Her family Is her priority. She is an introvert yet can make friends easily. She is very trustworthy and a sweet girl.

When removed from refrigerator ice changes to water,
Soil changes colour due to the properties of water...
Milk turns to curd by a drop of lemon,
A small change can make a saint turn into a demon
Going to the in-laws; the girls adapt so well,
How harder it be; although difficult to tell...
The angan where they spent their years,
The pain of its separation can't flow well through tears...
Yet they grow to a better individual,
And accept the home as if they belonged their skull...
A mother is a stage ahead in life,
Giving birth to a child; isn't it difficult to smile?
But that's how things should go,
As emotions are how we allow them to flow...
Like pain attracts pain a bit more,
Similarly, happiness would bring Joys at your door

It took days for him to make his home,
Although small it was his comfort zone
And then came to a broom rushing on the wall,
Broke his home and spider took a great fall...
He lost his everything in a spark of light,
Yet to survive; he did not stop his fight...
He ran around and found a corner to hide,
Started to build a new home keeping his sorrow aside...
Looking at the efforts the small creatures take,
Shouldn't we humans give more than we take?
As pain and gain go hand in hand,
So why not let positivity take a greater stand!

Giftson Jose

Giftson Jose is a passionate teacher from Kerala and also he works in various social service sectors and organizations.

Power of Positivity

When I look around,
I found the richest person in the world.

Down the street,
I saw a man who had no feet but wings.

So sad it happens,
Living lives in chains while we have the keys.

Live in the gutter of lost,
Casting hope as to touch the hopeful sky.

Bare of owns self-positivity,
A journey made by acceptance of who you are.

In the cloud of enthusiasm,
Open up the passage of your heart to chance.

Losses are not counted,
But entirely sure chances are been recounted.

All World is Paradise,
But It's up to you to load the real beauty of dice.

Vishali. S

Vishali was a literature student. She wants to use all opportunities to achieve her goals. She loves her mom to the core of the world. She wants to learn many things to enhance her skills. She loves to travel to other countries. She trusts herself one day she can achieve something in the world.

Everyone is born to achieve something in the world. Few of the people who are innovative and achieve their goals. Arise to achieve. Don't be lazy to live in an amazing world. We are born to win. We make any records before we die. We create our own identity of we lived in the world. Compete with your obstacles one day it is a potential for success. Set your dream goal work for it every day, every minute, every second of your life. Run, Run fast if not the people climb away and walk for their life. There are more negative people who discourage you and find your mistakes. Don't care about their words, just put away their swords and work for your dreams. Dream big is possible for all people but work hard is impossible, so break that impossible into possible. You are the effervescent person for you. Don't always be cranky. Just enjoy your life as you like. you are in a perilous situation although you need to bounce back from your dreams. Don't be petrified of your struggles. You have a wonderful fragile in your hand that is your aspirations. Life is too short so use your precious life without wasting time. Your destiny is created by you so change your destiny as you want. Trust yourself, be positive thought make you positive. Be confident in yourself. Every little effort of you use to reach your destination. Work hard, try your best, trust yourself, be positive one day u can win.

Rashmi Baweja

रश्मी इस कहानी की लेखिका बिल्कुल अपने नाम के अनुरूप ही सबके जीवन को प्रकाशित करती है। रश्मी हरियाणा के सोनीपत जिले की निवासी है। उन्होंने MCA किया है। उन्होंने अपना लेखन कार्य 2016 में प्रारंभ किया। वे बहुत ही स्पष्ट वादी है।वे फेसबुक पर HEART TOUCHING पेज पर भी लिखती हैं।https://www.facebook.com/rashmibaweja1993/अलग अलग विषयों पर वे बहुत अच्छा लिखती हैं। उनकी रचनाएँ पढ़कर दिल को सुकून मिलता है।

मुश्किलो को देखकर रुका नही हूँ मैं

मुश्किलो को देखकर कभी रुका नही हूँ मैं।
मंजिल को कह दो अभी थका नही हूँ मैं।
राह में अभी अंधेरा है तो क्या हुआ।
बता दो इन अंधेरो को डरा नही हूँ मै।।

रास्तो से कह दो मंज़िल दूर है तो क्या हुआ।
अपने कदम आगे बढ़ाने से रुका नही हूँ मैं।
मंज़िल नही दिख रही अभी मुझे तो क्या हुआ।
कह दो इनसे अभी रास्ते से भटका नही हूँ मैं।।

जितने इम्तिहान लेने है तुमने तुम ले लो।
क्योंकि इम्तिहान से मैं डरा नही हूँ कभी।
मेरी हिम्मत का तगाज़ा तुम मत लगाओ।
क्योंकि मेरे सब्र का बाँध टूटा नही है।।

दिल मे बसी है मंज़िल को पाने की चाहत।
चाहत से कह दो मोहब्बत अभी बदली नही है।
वो मुझसे बहुत दूर है तो क्या हो गया।
उसे पाने की चाहत अभी खत्म नही हुई है।।

Shivani Bhardwaj

Student
Melophile

Sometimes things go wrong,
When we go uphill our footsteps
Automatically tramp;
When you wanna smile,
But you have to groan.
When you have the opportunity
But you have to pay yourself for responsibilities.
When care exists, you flow it.
Rest if you must,
But you don't have to quit.
Life is full of surprises.
Having twist and turns hurdles.
As like everyone tackles and learn something.
Some people think he failure,
And those who have a strong desire to face it.

They become a warrior of the life.
Never give up!
I think this time you become low.
You may next time succeed with another blow.
Never give up! Someone say...
Success is failure turned inside and you never can tell how close you are. It can be very near when you afar from it.
You have to win Conquering positively

Jayashree Sahoo

Jayashree Sahoo is an habitant of Odisha.

Her writings started on yourquote, notojo, and mirakee like writing platforms. You can search her on yourquote by name of Jaya Jayashree. Nowadays She is a member of many writing communities and earned lots of certificates through her writings.

She is a co-author of 160+ anthologies. Also She is a Compiler of many anthologies in Hindi, English, and Odia languages. Currently, She is working as project head and board member of a reputed publication .

Wining Does Not Matter, Hardwork Matters

Always we should do hard work,
Don't expect for result and for winning,
If you doing strong hard work,
You must win
No one there aginst you there,
But if you don't do hard work,
Only if you live in dreaming,
Just hoping always that without doing nothing,
I'm sure to get success and I'll win,
It never happens,
Because for achieving success and winning
We have to do our work hard being strong and patient.

S. Vasha Varthini

A creative person with optimistic vibes. Working as an assistant professor in English. Love to learn new things. Provoke of thought penned as poems

Courageous Conquer

Do you know? You are a conquer person on earth.
Do you know? How is it possible?
Little fact of life
Just turn to watch
Ur courageous
....
There is a large number of sperm counts. Release inside the body
Many sperm dies in a way
Few reaches near the egg
Only one.
That is you fetched inside to become you.
Did you realize that how courageous a thing you did before you were born?
Without a hand without a leg. Without a mind and a heart.
Do u think now u cannot succeed with all this in you?
U can do everything. Be courageous conquer
Always...
Conquer beats you best...

Sarbani Dey

This is Sarbani Dey from Assam. Studying B.Sc in Maths. Having a great interest in writing poems and alongside she is a trained singer. Loves to spend her time nurturing her hobbies.

ज़िन्दगी है
दौर की मैदान नहीं,
तो हार जीत की फिकर मत करो ना।।
ज़िन्दगी तुम्हारी है
दुसरो के नहीं,
तो कौन क्या कहे वो मत सोचो ना।।
ज़िन्दगी है
पेड़ के तरह,
कभी ढेड़ सारा ख़ुशी तो कभी गम।।
दो पल की तो ये है ज़िन्दगी,
क्या पता कल हो ना हो,
तो अपने हर एक पल को खुशी से जीयो ना।।

Deepjyoti Chowdhury

Deepjyoti Chowdhury embraces reading and writing as her escape from the real world as well as a window to it. She is a strong believer in Christ and Karma. Currently pursuing a Master's in English literature, she has written in 100+ anthologies, she is the author of "Heartfelt musings" and "The staircase to freedom". Her main aim is to heal people and make them smile through her art of writing. You can follow her on Instagram at dj_writes_to_heal .

The Travel

I've traveled a long way to find myself,
And discover the hidden special features.
Throughout under Almighty's guidance,
Yes! I required lectures and counsel.

It's a long road and we might get lost,
The unending journey might get you exhaust.
Right choices will hike your cost,
Not immediately but gradually would be endorsed.

You would face trials and tribulations,
But you have to deal with utmost patience.
Challenges will hit you in an uneven sequence,
Your determination will give you winning assurance.

Falling is okay but stand again upright,
After the struggle, you would be under the spotlight.
The dark season might blind your sight,
But victory will make your life again bright.

Yamini Sona Vaishnavi

Yamini Sona Vaishnavi is a budding writer who pursues her III UG of English Literature in Madurai, Tamil Nadu. She has a great love for playing with words and a passion for reading and writing, especially poetry and quote writing. She is currently co-author of so many anthologies and wishes to write more. She started writing from her school days, where she used to contribute to the yearly magazine and continued the same in her college too. She wishes to touch the hearts of the readers through her poetry.

Pulverizing your fear :

Many a man dies of snake bites, says stories!
But, many men actually die of fear of snakes states the fact!
This invisible black evil fear is the cause of restriction!
Restriction for success coming your way, victory entering your home,
You top-scoring the mankind and conquering the entire earth!
History's legend's stories do we hear to get inspired and learn life lessons!
He who rules the land and people's heart is said to be a king!
Yet to be a king is not that easy, for you have to rule your own self!
Ruling one's own self is a hard nut to crack because it's merely a war!
A war, that goes on a battlefield called your soul for days together,
between your heart and the fear which has penetrated through it!
It may take a few days or months for some and a lifetime for many,
for this battle to come to an end, yet, ultimately, when,
Your heart wins over the fear that was pulling you back,
making you unstoppable now, and realize that this is how pulverizing fear feels!

Amritanshu Shreshth

Master Amritanshu Shreshth is a student of Open Minds A Birla School Kankarbagh, Patna, Bihar std. 9 with an excellent academic performance and a distinguished skill in sports. With a magnificent start at the age of 12, he is an avid writer with a keen interest in life lessons and classical literature with some specific hobbies like playing guitar. He loves to express his feelings and life lessons with his write-ups. He had won many medals and certificates in Literature and Debates with his writing and speaking skills and had written many articles and science documentaries with his pen name Yuvraj.

Win Over Barriers

If life is a race then adversities are its huddles and if life is a write-up then problems are its mistakes. Barriers are not more than a mere thinking of fear regarding something that is not possible for you to do at that stage of life but might be possible for you in the future as a result of your hard work and skills. Let barriers be no more than an illusion as they may change after a period of time and you keep overcoming each of them. They are no more than a small stone in life race but can be as massive as a mountain if thought of.

As it is truly said by Michelle Obama, "It's important for you to understand that your experience facing and overcoming adversity is actually one of the biggest advantages". You can even imagine different barriers as destinations rather than obstructions because the huddles are the only stepping stone to success as they direct you towards your goal and nowhere else. Everyone in their life face adverse conditions but people who take them as challenges only achieve success. This life combat can be made an obstruction less ground by the inner strength of the person. So, make life a barrier less combat by changing the barriers as your destination to achieve with strong determination and strength. Conquer the world like a king but remember to act like a joker in front of a group of idiots because it's not worthy to showcase of talent in front of jokers.

Write-up, quotes, poem and parental motivation will only work if you have a deep sense of self-motivation because the motivation could only help you to keep moving but self-motivation and determination will help you to overcome the life barriers and achieve success with flying colours. So, let these pity barriers no more than an illusions and jump over it without wasting time at these mere adversities in life. Find your goal and achieve it but it can be possible if you stop seeing the path but have your eyes at you goal.

Abhilash Sharma

Abhilash Sharma a 23 year old passionate writer. He belongs to Sonipat , Haryana . He had completed his B.com (voc) recently. He is a enthusiastic person and a sports lover as well .Worked as a co author in about 40+ anthologies inspired by Ishika Arora and Ishani Aggarwal in the field of writing .You can check out his writings on instagram at @ankahe_alfaaz_ .

विजय :- एक संघर्ष की कहानी

एक संघर्ष की कहानी ,
जो हो चली है अब पुरानी ,
मिसाले है जिसकी सबको सुनानी ,
हो चली दुनिया अब उसकी दीवानी ,

दुनिया ने उसे गिराया था ,
वो भी एक दिन लड़खड़ाया था ,
ना जाने क्यों इतना डराया था ,
किसे ने ना उसे उठाया था ,

बस मन में एक बार ठाना था ,
उसको अपनी जंग जो माना था ,
अब तो बस कर दिखाना था ,
परचम जो लहराना था ।।

Sadhana Singh

A lover of books and nature, paints the various colours of life.

छोड़ती जा रही हूँ , मैं पीछे अपने धीरे- धीरे रिश्तों को
क्युंकि झुक गए हैं मेरे कंधे बोझ से इनके
अब हल्का होना चाहती हूँ"
"दुखों का बाजार मत लगाइये जनाब
यहाँ इनका खरिद्दार नहीं मिलता"
"कसमें झूठी, झूठे वादे
सच्ची एक कोशिश तेरी"
"वो चल दिए दिल के टुकड़े टुकड़े करके
मुड़ कर भी ना देखा
और हमने ज़िंदगी गुज़ार दी
उन टुकड़ों को जोड़ने में"
"बदलाव की बात यहाँ न कीजिये
यह मुर्दों की बस्ती है
आपके नारों का शोर सन्नाटा लिख जायेगा
यह मुर्दों की बस्ती है"

"ये ज़िंदगी बहुत छोटी है नफ़रत के लिए
ज़रा संभल कर खर्च करना
यूँ ना हो की गुज़र जाए ज़िंदगी तमाम नफ़रत में
एक कोना प्यार के लिए बचा कर रखना"

"मासूम है दिल अपना बच्चों सा
मुस्कुरा दो तो माफ कर देते हैं
शिकायत रहती नहीं किसी से हमको
बस नाराज़गी का नकाब ही ओढ़ पाते हैं
नफ़रत करने वालों को सलाम
कुछ और करने आता नहीं हमको
हम तो बस प्यार ही कर पाते हैं"

"चलते- चलते थक जाती हूँ
की ज़रा छाव मिल तो थम जाऊँ
पल दो पल को
रास्ता लम्बा है बहुत
की ज़रा साथ मिले तो खिल जाऊँ
पल दो पल को"

Shivani Batra

Shivani Batra is pursuing MSc in Biotechnology from Amity University, Noida. Her poems are about living an optimistic life and competing with the failures like a warrior because they are just part of your life.

When the path taken to cross the river,
Pebbles will always know you better,
Hurdles will keep you away
But the dreams are important to chase
If the surface is smooth objects will slide,
So speed breakers are necessary too, to build a successful life
Conquer the world but remember your roots,
Battles are hard to fight, saddest and even depressed phases are just a part of life
You are not alone, your loved ones are there always by your side.
The world will be a better place hopes are mine
Even the Sun has to burn in order to shine.

Lakshmi Soni

This is Lakshmi. She's belongs to the Maharashtra. She's a passionate writer. Kalam and paintbrush gave wings to her words. She writes to express her feelings and imaginations.

Apni nakamiyo ko tu simat le zara
Unhe ummidon ke dhage me piro le zara
Moti moti jod kar mehnat tu kar zara
Khun pasina ek karke tu chingarri sa bhadak tho zara
Ek ashiyaana apna basa tho zara
Bikhre hua kwab ko fir bana tho zara
Tu apne aap me khud ko khoj tho zara ek katra tere khun ka tu shyahi bana tho zara
Tute huye guitar se sur nikal tho zara tu bekhwab ud tho zara
Ek nagma kamiyabi ka likh tho zara
Tu khud pr Fateh kar tho zara......

Keshav Tibrewal

Keshav Tibrewal is an accidental writer from Bhubaneswar, Odisha. He is a part-time poet who creates something new only when he experiences something. His journey of writing was impossible without his mentors Anshuman Mohanty and Tejaswinee Nayak. Connect with him on Instagram- @_tibrewal.

An Apple

Buying an apple or getting it from somewhere to eat is a mere task for us. It takes absolutely nothing to throw it if we don't like it... Right?

On my way to my village, I had nothing but four apples to eat. I never liked eating fruits while traveling, so I kept them for my grandmother.
And when she was eating, she told me to offer one to our driver.

At first, it was awkward for me... To give an apple to a "driver", but then I thought what's the point of throwing it when I reach, so it's better that he eats.

And just because he didn't eat anything in the morning and it was 2 by that time... I offered him the apple.

Then I went for a nap, and around 5 we reached our place.

Our driver had to leave the car with us and travel around 30 km more to reach his native place.

While taking out the luggage, I saw that he was putting an apple inside his bag. I enquired and got to know that he didn't eat the apple that I gave him rather kept it for his son. He was hungry the whole day for his son's happiness.

And obviously, it's natural that you wait to see your father after months and are curious to know what he brought for you. His son might feel the same. And then I realized how important that single apple could be, for changing his day.

I was trying to control my emotions and all I could do is to give him 2 more apples that were left with me... Because, I being a rich brat, didn't like apples while traveling.

The whole night I was trying to imagine the expressions of his son, the reason being that fruits are luxury for them.

And I realized, that, big things don't make a difference, but small efforts do.
A mere fruit that is absolutely useless for us is enough to make someone's day, all it takes is a small effort.

The next time I refuse to eat something, or the next time I throw something... I'll definitely think about the level of satisfaction I get by giving it to someone who values it more than I do.

Anand Jain

ANAND JAIN is a good writer from FAZILKA, PUNJAB.
He has completed his GRADUATION in commerce stream. From Panjab University.
He has been writing poetry for 3 years as his passion. With the help of my sister (Sapna Jain) and brother (Rakesh Jain).
He wants to be a successful banker in the future.
He is a founder of ROBIN HOOD ARMY, FAZILKA (NGO).

बात

इस सियासत से खुद को बचाओ, तब कोई बात बने
सोचो, समझो, दिमाग़ लगाओ, तब कोई बात बने

सच कहता हूं, इंसानियत बिना तुम मुर्दा हो
ऊपर वाले को ज़मीं पे लाओ, तब कोई बात बने

मोहब्बत में तो गले लगाना सबको आता है
मोहब्बत से भी गले लगाओ, तब कोई बात बने

कब तलक होगी यू ही लाशों पे राजनीति?
अपनी भी ताक़त दिखाओ, तब कोई बात बने

गोली, कट्टा, मार-काट ये कब तक होगा?
सत्य अहिंसा याद दिलाओ, तब कोई बात बने ।

औकात

एक माचिस की तिल्ली,
एक घी का लोटा, लकड़ियों के ढेर पे, कुछ घण्टे में राख...
बस इतनी-सी है, आदमी की औकात!!!

एक बूढा बाप शाम को मर गया, अपनी सारी ज़िन्दगी, परिवार के
नाम कर गया... कहीं रोने की सुगबुगाहट, तो कहीं फुसफुसाहट...
अरे जल्दी ले जाओ, कौन रोयेगा सारी रात...
बस इतनी-सी है, आदमी की औकात!!!

मरने के बाद नीचे देखा, नज़ारे नज़र आ रहे थे, मेरी मौत पे...
कुछ लोग ज़बरदस्त, तो कुछ ज़बरदस्ती
रो रहे थे... नहीं रहा... चला गया... चार दिन करेंगे बात.
बस इतनी-सी है, आदमी की औकात!!!

बेटा अच्छी तस्वीर बनवायेगा,
सामने अगरबत्ती जलाना, खुश्बुदार फूलों की माला होगी... अखबार
में अश्रुपूरित श्रद्धांजलि होगी...
बाद में उस तस्वीर पे,जाले भी कौन करेगा साफ़...
बस इतनी-सी है, आदमी की औकात!!!!
जिन्दगी भर, मेरा-मेरा-मेरा किया... अपने लिए कम,
अपनों के लिए ज्यादा जीया... कोई न देगा साथ... जायेगा खाली
हाथ...
क्या तिनका ले जाने की भी,
है हमारी औकात...???

Sarvesh Bagde

This is Sarvesh Bagde, Hailing from "The City of Oranges", Nagpur.
He is a student of life sciences.
Writing is his passion and he is penning for the last 5 years.
He loves writing Quotes, articles, some short stories, etc.
You can read his writings here
Blogs-https://sarveshbagde.blogspot.com/?m=1
YourQuote-https://www.yourquote.in/sarveshbagde

अनंत असीम उचाइयो में
मैं सपने लेकर निकला हूँ ।
तोड़कर सारी ज़ंजीरें
मैं आज उड़ने निकला हूँ ।

चाहे फेको मुझपे जितने कंकड़
उन्हें सहेज में अपनी ढाल बनाऊँगा ।
करलो चाहे जितनी कोशिश
मै फिर उभरकर आऊँगा ।।1।।

मन में है अरमान कई
उन सबको मुझे अब पाना है ।
सीमाओं से बांधा दुनिया ने अब तक
पर अब हद से गुज़र जाना है ।

मृत्यु का मुझे अब भय नहीं
मै तूफानों से भी लड़ जाऊँगा ।
अपनी मंज़िल को हाथों में लेकर
मै फिर उभरकर आऊँगा ।।2।।

इस जग में जितने जुल्म नहीं
उतने सेहने की ताक़त है ।
झुकने का मुझे शौक नहीं
सच कहने की मुझे आदत है ।

हालातो की ज्वलंत भट्टी में भी
मैं सहज ही कूद जाऊँगा
तप तपकर सोना बनकर
मै फिर उभरकर आऊँगा ।।3।।

Bhavika Dhiraj Sindhi

Bhavika Dhiraj Sindhi a 25-year-old
creative writer.
She belongs to Turkey an Indian writing from abroad due to her passion for writing.
A B.Com graduate.
She is writing since 7th std.
But has now started collaborating for Writing.

Life:- A Bag Full Of Uncertain Road

Try making life into a daring adventure...
Life is what you make of it
It's not a rehearsal but it's the main event...
So, plan as you gonna live forever
But...
Love as if u gonna die tomorrow...
People will come and go...
Don't you worry some days there could be a war between positive and negative...
But it's okay to go through such a phase...
In the middle of difficulties lies an opportunity just grab it whenever you can...
Don't quit
Take a leave breathe travel or do whatever makes you calm...
But never let you break...
Taking learning lessons may not make you weak rather you can climb the mountains better...
Make mistakes...
Because you are human and humans tend to make mistakes...
Never lose hope for that you failed today so you won't conquer give your best and you will definitely climb the stairs of success...
And you will surely do better than the rest...

Shivansh Sharma

He is Shivansh Sharma. Basically from Indore but persuing MBA (Marketing & HR) in Mysore Karnataka. He always has a passion for writing the thoughts which come into his mind. A hardcore foodie as he belongs to Indore. He is the one who is always ready to help his near ones. His life revolves around his family and friends. He is always self-motivated, enthusiastic and a person with positive vibes. He is co-author of 20+ books and a compiler of 1 book.

सकारात्मकता

चल उठ और खड़ा हो,
कब तक मायूस रहेगा,
कब तक घूट घूट कर जीयेगा,
कुछ नया सीख कुछ नया कर,
कल का क्यूं सोच रहा है तू,
जो करना है आज कर,
जो आज है उसको जाने मत दे,
जो चला गया उसका मत सोच,
थोड़ा भीड़ से अलग चल,
थोड़ी ज्यादा मेहनत कर,
जब तक मंज़िल पास ना लगे
अपने कर्म करते चल,
चल, उठ कुछ नया कर,
अपनी अलग पहचान से मुकाम हासिल कर,
अपने आलस को हटा और
कुछ हट कर अपना मुकाम हासिल कर,
इतना मत सोच की मंज़िल दूर है,
पर इतनी भी पास नहीं की आसानी से मिल जाए,
चल उठ भी जा और अपनी मंज़िल हासिल कर,
क्यूंकि कोशिश करने वालो की हार ने होती,
कुछ ना मिला तो अनुभव मिलेगा,
हारा तो कुछ भी नहीं है पर जीत बहुत कुछ ज्येगा,
चल उठ और कुछ नया कर,
आराम से पर कुछ हट कर अपना मुकाम हासिल कर,

Archana Paryani

Archana Paryani - She is a fervent fan of honor loyalty and chivalry. She brings life in the world where men and women stand shoulder to shoulder, steady in the desire to make the world a better place for all.

She is a small-town girl with big big dream. She is the perfect mixture of sweetheart and warrior.

She is a finance professional with a passion for writing.

Instagram handle : little_love_left

It's all about
Either Do or die
Choice is yours

Be a mystery
To create your own "History"

Swords are made by heating iron
Diamonds are cut n shaped by a steel blade
So now when you're pressurized
Turn to a sword to kill the negatives and shine and glitter like a diamond..

अभी भी वक़्त है,

जो देखे थे सपने ,
बना लो उन्हें अपने,
एक बार जो ये वक़्त जायेगा,
फिर लौट कर कभी नहीं आएगा,

उनकी दुआ का असर एक दिन जरूर होगा,
माँ का वो छोटा सा बच्चा एक दिन जरूर कामयाब होगा,

जब रात बहुत गहरी हो जाए ना...
तो समझ लेना के सवेरा होने में अब ज्यादा वक़्त नहीं है।

Christy Gnana Deepa. J

Proudly presenting our writer, Christy Gnana Deepa, 20, hailing from Tamil Nadu, India, and now residing in Madurai for her studies. She is pursuing an undergraduate in English literature at Fatima College, Madurai.

Her journey to date is amazing by being a compiler of 4 anthologies and a co-author of more than 30+ anthologies. A writer by passion and a literarian by profession. You can follow her on Instagram (___budding___writer) for more writeups.

Positivity

HAIKU

1. DAWN

Brightening dawn,
Early morning strength,
Wakes me up like an alarm.

2.NATURE

Sit quietly,
To admire the beauty,
Your beauty grows by itself.

3. TIME

Great blessing and a gift
Can change everything when you
Use it wisely.

Ipsita Panigrahi

A carefree, joyful, realistic in practical life but she enjoys living in an imaginative and fictional world. This is Ipsita Panigrahi, a budding writer, who loves to express her feelings and emotions through writings. She hails from Bhubaneswar - the city of temples, Odisha. She has a passion for literature, as she loves to do all those stuff that makes her happy and literature is one among them. She is likely to be called a scribbler. She finds peace in gardening and reading books and an artist is also hidden in her.

Start

Start now.
Start from where you are.
Start with fear.
Start with eyes filled with tears.
Start no matter day or night.
Start if you want to become wright.
Start with shaking hands.
Start with a trembling voice.
Start with what you have.
Start for what you want.
Start with doubts.
Start for becoming the one among the crowd.
Start with hesitation.
Start with restrictions.
Start with scars.
Start to become the star.
Don't stop... don't quit.
Just start... and stop after,
Getting what you dreamt for,
What you wished for.

Urja Motwani

Urja Motwani a 21-year-old writer she has completed her BMM. She is a fashion and travel enthusiast and loves to write about her feelings.

You Are Worth It, My Love

Your words, your thoughts is what you're mind believes in give it more love
No matter the struggle you faced the other day make it positive because it benefits you because in the future it makes you who you are
Take your learnings and keep your head high love
Your mistakes are forgiven if you choose to forgive them in your mind
Your world is you because at the end of the day you have to live with it
A person can try to comfort you give you love, care about you but till the time you don't forgive till the time it's in your head it won't affect you much or maybe for a time being it may do but it won't last long
I just wanna say you are worth all the love care and happiness in this world
The words of others may affect you but your kind words to yourself and the journey inside you will count the most the days unhappy inside makes harder for you to survive & the days happy inside makes you kinder happier & most of all it will make your perspective wider & you will be able to understand people and not judge them so choose to be happy inside
Because you are worth it, my love.

R. Susanna Celsia

Passionate writer, blogger, poet, who has published a solo book titled " Oasis of Poetry" who writes with a blend of reality and fiction.

Between The Lines

From a young age, I was taught what was success looked like and what it didn't look like, and no one knows if it was even right or not. As days went by I wondered why? And how these actually began and why do we inherit this and why do we pass this on horizontally and vertically! The answer is still unknown.

Being in the spotlight is called success at times and when the same star is unhappy and sad and cry themselves at night, is it even worth being in the spotlight and have a broken soul? Like using dollars to mend a broken heart! Which doesn't happen.

When poor labour is working hard, someone once told me, work hard !! Don't become like him !! I wondered, why not? He has a smile and his family loves him !! Success is relative they say, is it so I wondered? Is it just comparing the amount of money, my bank has with another ? and feel better and tag myself successful. Or is it just that good vibe when few mouths applaud me? Is it just doing everything to earn those words from people and so-called " respect ", isn't every human being due respect?

Now I feel success doesn't exist at all!!

Life is more than standards, money, and what people think. It's about living your life to the fullest and living your purpose.

Ponmitha Selvaraj

Ponmitha Selvaraj is a passionate writer, who writes quotes and random stuff. She strives to become the best writer, she is pursuing Literature in Fatima College, Madurai. She posts her writeups on her Instagram page starred_lines and yourquote.

Positivity

People asked for,

Much of positivity and ended up having much in other.

Much of adventure and ended up in staying home for covid adventure

Much of new hopes and ended up in new kinds of prayers.

Much of magics and ended up in many masks. Much of victories in real and ended up online for everything:(simply no words)

Much of giggles and ended up in much of home gossips.

Much in everything when 2020 started and ended up having so much than we asked for too less from it. Ok. Ok. Let's hope for optimism

Let it be the last day of suffering and pains and yeah cheer up for the happy beginning !!!!

Dhiraj Sindhi

Dhiraj Sindhi a 30 year old man..
A person all day at work
And night thoughts all he land up in writing and washing away all of them...
Because keeping in his creates a burden and becomes difficult to work next day so he chooses to write down...

Conquering Fear

My exams were near
I was full of fear
I studied late night for my answers to be right...
I was frightened like ever..
Because I knew I wasn't clever..
I couldn't sleep a wink..
Just think think and think...
If I wouldn't pass
I would be in the same class
Next day was creepy
And I was sleepy...
On the exam table I tried to be stable
I was in shock to see the clock
For I was sleeping all through the silly exams...
And I failed....
All depressed cursing myself...
The one who didn't let me fall
my mother helped me to win...
I was in the same class...
While my friends in the other..
I started studying daily...
My mother helped me survive with this fear...
Thank you is alll I can tell her to have her near...
Collecting each drop of honey
And finally I made a honeycomb...
Same way my exams were near...
I just revised and slept...
For my anxiety was calm...
This time I had no fear
The other day was the exam
And I finally wrote my exams
This year I finally promised my mother
To conquer my fear...

Flairs and Glairs, a platform by a student for the students. We are esteemed youth struggling to carve out our path for our future and we follow a basic mindset Since everyone is not born with all-round skills. Joining hands with people who are born to execute it with perfection is the best way to evolve. Self-Evolution is the need of the hour but, evolving as a community is what we strive for. The initiative as kickstarted by, Founder- Mr. Shubham Shah with the motive to utilize the skillset and talent of writing has now a team of 10+ people who are actively participating into newer forms of learning and discovering talents among youngsters. We Provide platform and services like Publishing opportunities, Open mics, Workshops, Hands-on training. Operating with Brand Name of Flairs and Glairs (Publication House), we offer the chance of elevating a passionate writer to an esteemed author With Brand name Teekhe Zasbaaat. We bring to you an opportunity to get accustomed with the Public Speaking and Presenting of Thoughts along with regular challenges to brush up your inking spirit. The newest initiative to extend our services we introduced in a new writing Platform- The Glittering Fables and Ink Over Tears.

We Choose to Fly Like A Falcon than to be a

Leg Pulling Crab.

To Know More: Infoline – 7781900870
Mail Us At-
flairsandglairs@gmail.com / info@flairsandglairs.in
Or Visit is at
www.flairsandglairs.com / www.flairsandglairs.in
Social Handles- @flairsandglairs @teekhezasbaaat

www.ingramcontent.com/pod-product-compliance
Ingram Content Group UK Ltd.
Pitfield, Milton Keynes, MK11 3LW, UK
UKHW022005190726
13853UKWH00004B/1747

9 789390 799114